DOGPARK:
The Musical

by Jahnna Beecham, Malcolm Hillgartner & Michael J. Hume

Songs by Malcolm Hillgartner

Vocal Arrangements by Malcolm Hillgartner & Chip Duford

A SAMUEL FRENCH ACTING EDITION

SAMUEL FRENCH

FOUNDED 1830

NEW YORK HOLLYWOOD LONDON TORONTO

SAMUELFRENCH.COM

ISBN 978-0-573-69744-9   Printed in U.S.A.   #29187

RENTAL MATERIALS

An orchestration consisting of a **Conductor's Score**, **Piano**, **Guitar**, **Reeds** and **Vocal Chorus Books** will be loaned two months prior to the production ONLY on the receipt of the Licensing Fee quoted for all performances, the rental fee and a refundable deposit. In addition, theatres that cannot support live accompaniment, a CD of music accompaniment is available for rehearsal and performance use.

Please contact Samuel French for perusal of the music materials as well as a performance license application.

IMPORTANT BILLING AND CREDIT REQUIREMENTS

All producers of *DOGPARK: THE MUSICAL must* give credit to the Author of the Play in all programs distributed in connection with performances of the Play, and in all instances in which the title of the Play appears for the purposes of advertising, publicizing or otherwise exploiting the Play and/or a production. The name of the Author *must* appear on a separate line on which no other name appears, immediately following the title and *must* appear in size of type not less than fifty percent of the size of the title type.

DOGPARK premiered January 9, 2009 in the Stackner Cabaret of the Milwaukee Repertory Theater (Sandy Ernst, Stackner Cabaret director/ associate artistic director; Joseph Hanreddy, artistic director). The director was Jahnna Beecham, the music director was Malcolm Hillgartner, the choreographer was Suzanne Seiber, the stage manager was Mark S. Sahba, the assistant stage manager was Elizabeth Barnes, the scenic design was by Susannah M. Barnes, the costumes were designed by Holly Payne, with lights by Aimee Hanyzenski and props by James Guy. The cast was as follows:

DAISY .... Katherine Strohmaier
ITCHY .... Jonathan Spivey
CHAMP .... Lenny Banovez
BOGIE .... Chip Duford

CHARACTERS

DAISY is a slightly neurotic but sassy Westie. Although she's been burned by guys before, she's still looking for Mr. Gooddog.

CHAMP is a purebred Collie. Charming, handsome, and he knows it. He's a show dog, done a commercial or two. Lots of brawn but very little brain.

ITCHY is the goofball sidekick with a list of phobias as long as your arm. Quick with the lip, he's the first to challenge, and the first to roll over on his back and confess, "Just kiddin'."

BOGIE is a streetwise Lab/mix with a dark secret. He "sticks his neck out for nobody."

MUSICAL ACCOMPANIMENT

For theatres that cannot support live accompaniment, a CD of music accompaniment is available for rehearsal and performance use. For more information, please contact Samuel French, Inc.

For Sandy Ernst and Joe Hanreddy
New plays would not exist without champions. Thank you for being ours.

ACT ONE

(Four dogs in silhouette: A Westie, a Collie, a Jack Russell terrier, and a lab mutt.)

SONG 1: DOGPARKAPELLA

ALL.

IN THE HEART OF THIS TOWN
THERE'S A SHANGRI-LA,
A SWEET LITTLE ACRE OF GREEN.
A FANTASY LAND WITH A POOL AND GREAT PLAY TOYS.
I GO THERE TO RUN AND TO BE SEEN

DAISY.

IF YOU'RE LOOKING FOR ROMANCE
THIS PLACE MIGHT BE EDEN

ALL.

AND IT'S OPEN FROM MORNING TIL DARK
IT'S HEAVEN!
VALHALLA!
IT'S OVER THE RAINBOW
THIS PLACE THAT WE LOVE –
DOGPARK!

(Lights up on **ITCHY**, *a Jack Russell terrier.)*

(SFX: Whistle, male voice: "Itchy. Walkies!")

ITCH. Oh boy! You're the greatest!

(Lights up on **CHAMP**, *a Collie.)*

(SFX: male voice: "Champ! In the car.")

CHAMP. I'm right beside you, pal.

(Lights up on **DAISY**, *a Westie.)*

(SFX: female voice: "Daisy. Dogpark!")

DAISY. Wait, I'm not ready!

> (*SFX: female voice: "We promised ourselves we'd give it one chance. And if it didn't work out, we wouldn't go back."*)

DAISY. (*to audience*) We? There was no "we."

> (*SFX: female voice: "Now Daisy, You need to get out and make friends before all your fur falls out."*)

> (*to audience*) I have a nervous condition. Perfectly normal for a Westie.

> (*SFX: female voice: "Daisy, we're going to Lovers with Leashes. And that's all there is to it!"*)

> (*to audience*) Lovers with Leashes? Kinky.

SONG #2: TODAY'S THE DAY

TODAY IS THE DAY,
SHE'S MAKING ME GO OUT AND PLAY,
I JUST CAN'T HIDE ANYMORE.

YES, TODAY IS THE DAY,
I LIVE MY LIFE A DIFFERENT WAY,
NOW WATCH ME WALK RIGHT OUT THE DOOR!

I'VE BEEN THROUGH ALL THOSE POSERS,
ALL THOSE NOSERS TAKING SNIFFS.
THEY SAY LET'S WALK, I WANNA TALK,
BUT THEY JUST WANT A WHIFF.

BUT TODAY'S A NEW DAY!
I WON'T BE SAYING NAY, NO WAY!
IT'S TIME TO MEET THE NEW DAISY!

ITCHY.

TODAY'S THE DAY, MY TIME IS NOW,
THE ITCH MACHINE WILL SHOW THEM HOW,
I'M NOT THE RUNT, I'M NOT THE CLOWN
TODAY I TURN THIS GAME AROUND.

I'LL SHOW THAT PACK, THOSE MUTTS WHO LACK
MY CHARM, CHARISMA – OH MY GOD!

(*Notices he's in a sweater.*)

ITCHY. *(cont.)*

WHAT IS THIS? I'M SUCH A FRAUD!

NO BABE IS GONNA HAVE A FLING
WITH A DOG IN A SWEATER, I MEAN, WHERE'S THE ZING?
NOW IT'S TOO LATE TO TURN AROUND,
TO THAT DOGPARK I'M BOUND.

CHAMP.

TODAY IS THE DAY!
EVERYTHING'S GONNA COME MY WAY,
IT'S ONLY FAIR, I'M PEDIGREED.

YES, TODAY IS THE DAY!
YOU LADIES, BETTER LOOK MY WAY,
I'M SATISFACTION, GUARANTEED.

IT'S NATURAL SELECTION,
IN THE GENES, DONCHA KNOW?
IF THIS WAS AN ELECTION
I'D BE VOTED BEST IN SHOW.

'CAUSE TODAY IS THE DAY!
YOU MUTTS AND STRAYS, GET OUTTA MY WAY,
HERE COMES THE BEST OF THE BREED.

*(During next exchange, **DAISY**, **CHAMP** and **ITCHY** "get in" cars.)*

(SFX: male voice: "Up, Champ! Good boy.")

*(**CHAMP** turns his "car" to face downstage; he's in the passenger seat next to driver.)*

(SFX: male voice: "Itchy, get in the back. The back!!")

*(**ITCHY** is in the backseat, running from window to window.)*

*(SFX: Female voice [á la David in Alvin and the Chipmunks]: "Daisy? Daisy? **DAISY**!!!")*

DAISY. OKAY!!! I'll go. But *I* get to drive.

(Daisy's in the "car," in the front on the driver's side.)

ITCHY.

> JUST A FEW SECONDS, A COUPLE OF FEET,
> FROM THE ELEVATOR DOWN TO THE STREET,
> SPIN IN A CIRCLE, I'M OUT THE DOOR,
> WHEELS DON'T FAIL ME NOW, IT'S ONLY 3 BLOCKS MORE!

ALL.

> TO THE DOGPARK!

DAISY.

> WHERE LOVE MIGHT COME MY WAY!

CHAMP. Which way?

ITCHY. This way!

CHAMP. Okay!

ALL.

> TO THE DOGPARK!

DAISY.

> WHERE LOVERS WITH LEASHES

ALL.

> ARE – TO – MEET TODAY.

DAISY.

> TODAY IS THE DAY!
> I THROW MYSELF INTO THE FRAY
> IT'S TIME FOR ME TO TAKE THE LEAD.

CHAMP/ITCHY. Yes it is, yes it is, indeed!

> YES, TODAY IS THE DAY!

CHAMP/ITCHY. Look out!

DAISY.

> I'M FINALLY ON MY WAY,
> THIS TIME I KNOW I WILL SUCCEED.

ITCHY.

> JUST FOLLOW MY DIRECTIONS
> AND WE'LL BE THE FIRST TO SHOW.

CHAMP.

> NO MORE PROCRASTINATIONS,
> HIT THE GAS! C'MON, LET'S GO!

DAISY.

> YES, TODAY IS THE DAY!

ITCHY. Hurray!

CHAMP.

> EVERY DOG'S GOTTA HAVE HIS SPECIAL DAY
> AND NO DOG'S SPECIAL-ER THAN ME!
>
> *(shouts)*
>
> Where'm I goin'?

ALL.

> TO THE DOGPARK!

ITCHY.

> TODAY'S THE DAY, MY TIME IS NOW!

ALL.

> THE DOGPARK!

ITCHY.

> THE ITCH MACHINE WILL SHOW THEM HOW!
> I'M ALPHA DOG, I'M THE HEAD OF THE PACK –
> YOU WON'T SEE ME LYIN' ON MY BACK
> TO SCRATCH MY SACROILIAC.

ALL.

> THE DOGPARK!

DAISY.

> I WON'T GIVE UP, I WON'T BACK DOWN!

ALL.

> THE DOGPARK!

DAISY.

> I ONCE WAS LOST BUT NOW I'M FOUND.
> YOU KNOW THE DOGPARK IS THE PLACE TO BE!

ALL.

> THE DOGPARK!

CHAMP.

> CAN'T BE LATE, I'VE GOT A DATE!

ALL.

> THE DOGPARK!

DAISY.

> IT'S JUST THE PLACE TO FIND A MATE!

ALL.

> THE DOGPARK –
> YOU AND –

*(As the cars arrive at the park, **CHAMP** and **ITCHY** spot each other and growl furiously at each other, then drop for last note.)*

DAISY. Get me out of here

ALL.

– ME!

*(Lights up on **BOGIE**. He carries a tattered jacket.)*

BOGIE. My park. I like it. The grass always looks like it's been left out all night. *(Crosses to the fire hydrant, he sets the jacket down.)* Today is the day when I… *(Crosses to the gate and looks out.)* Well, it's a day full of possibilities.

*(**CHAMP** and **ITCHY** offstage – their "let me out" and "offs" are audible.)*

ITCHY. *(offstage)* Let me out! Let me out!

CHAMP. *(starts offstage)* You park and I'll run on ahead.

(SFX: male voice, "Champ! The Frisbee.")

ITCHY. Bye, Best Friend Forever. And good-bye, sweater!

(Struggles making "arrgh arrgh" dog sounds trying to get it off. He fails.)

CHAMP. *(Shows he's got the Frisbee.)* I'm way ahead of you. Hey! Hey! Hey!

*(**CHAMP** and **ITCHY** run to the gate where **BOGIE** is now standing. To rap beat, they greet each other in an elaborate dog hello with sniffing and gestures to decide who's top dog.)*

ITCHY. Champ!

CHAMP. What's up, dawg? *(Drum beat begins.)*

ITCHY/CHAMP. My butt. Your butt.

ITCHY. Tight gut!

ITCHY/CHAMP. Head, head, neck, neck.

CHAMP. Short mutt.

ITCHY. Sniff, sniff.

CHAMP. Woo hoo!

ITCHY. Good pew!

CHAMP. Sniff, sniff.

ITCHY. Woo hoo!

CHAMP. You too!

ITCHY. Look at me, I'm on top!

CHAMP. Not for long, you milksop!

BOGIE. *(steps between them)* Back off boys, I say stop. I'm the one who's on top. Take a whiff. *(Drum beat stops.)* It's me! Top Dog!

(SFX: Oriental gong)

CHAMP/ITCHY. *(in awe)* Alpha guy!

BOGIE. All right, you're good to go. Come on in!

*(**CHAMP** and **ITCHY** enter, Champ circles the area on stage checking messages.)*

ITCHY. Hey, Bogie, where's your Best Friend Forever?

BOGIE. My BFF? He must be at the Clubhouse. Yeah, there he is. See?

ITCHY. Which one?

BOGIE. Ah, you missed him. He went inside.

ITCHY. Oh. Champ, throw me the Stick.

CHAMP. Hold on – I'm checking my pee-mail.

BOGIE. Catch this.

CHAMP. *(reading messages)* Princess says she'll be late.

ITCHY. *(squeezes toy)* The squeaker's gone.

CHAMP. Barney wants a Frisbee rematch. Loser.

ITCHY. *(still staring at toy)* Why?

BOGIE. *(answering **ITCHY**)* Some guys just want to ruin it for the rest of us.

ITCHY. That's just not right.

CHAMP. Mystic's at the dog whisperer.

BOGIE. Again?

ITCHY. *(Drops disgusting toy back in box. Goes to hand sanitizer.)* Sanitize.

(DAISY enters.)

DAISY. *(calling back offstage to BFF)* You may be my Best Friend Forever, but you don't have to push. *(to audience)* I would have gotten out of the car eventually. *(Bends over to adjust her boots.)*

(SFX: BOING! Sound of being hit with a skillet. Musical cue: Mendelsohn's "Spring" accompanies odor wafting across the fence.)

(All male dogs at full attention, noses in air.)

CHAMP. What is that aroma?

BOGIE. Cassis and cranberry – full-bodied and ripe!

ITCHY. I'm getting medium to dark notes –

CHAMP. And fresh cut grass.

BOGIE. With just a touch of Beggin' Strips.

(SFX: Timer Ding)

CHAMP/ITCHY. *(Freeze with noses in air.)* HOT DOG!

DAISY. *(Jolts to upright position.)* Uh, oh.

CHAMP & ITCHY. AH-OOOOOOOO!

*(**CHAMP** and **ITCHY** run to fence and talk at once. Their "heys" and "woos" continue to their next lines.)*

CHAMP. Ooh, baby! Come on in! Hey! Hey! Hey!

ITCHY. I'm starting to drool. Woo! Woo! Woo!

CHAMP. Watcha waiting for?

DAISY. They're animals.

ITCHY.	**CHAMP.**
Doggess, nymph divine! You like jokes? I got a million of 'em...	Champ – as in the one and only. Hey! Hey! Hey! Hey!

(Continues until his next line.)

ITCHY. ...A Corgi, a wombat and a cockroach walk into a pet store – stay with me. Stay with me...

DAISY. *(pulls away)* Personal space. Personal space!

ITCHY. Hey! Hey! Hey! Hey!... *(Continues until his next line.)*

CHAMP. I'm sure you know me. It's hard for a public dog to have a private life.

DAISY. *(Runs the other way.)* Ew! They're panting. I can't stand that!

ITCHY. ...Say, do you like balloon animals? AH-OOOOO!

CHAMP. Itchy, go chase your tail. Look at me. At meeeeeeeee!

DAISY. *(Confronts them.)* Does anyone here want to know my name?

CHAMP/ITCHY. *(Stop howling.)* Huh?

(**BOGIE** *pulls out a cat toy and squeezes it. It makes a "meow" sound.*)

CHAMP/ITCHY. Cat!!

(**BOGIE** *throws the cat toy offstage and* **CHAMP** *and* **ITCHY** *run after it.*)

DAISY. *(to audience)* Well. That was fun. *(Calls to BFF)* All right. Let's get back in the car!

BOGIE. *(to self)* Turn around and you'll be looking trouble square in the eye.

DAISY. *(calling to friend)* Yoo-hoo! BFF!

BOGIE. *(Spins and sees* **DAISY**. *Speaks to audience.)* Can't help myself. If I was a really bad dog, I'd be all over her like milk on a bone.

DAISY. *(calling to BFF)* Don't act like you can't hear me!

BOGIE. *(to* **DAISY***)* Say, are you coming or going?

DAISY. What? I don't know. *(aside to audience)* He's cute.

BOGIE. Look, I'm holding the gate. Either come in or get out.

DAISY. *(aside to audience)* Not THAT cute. *(back to* **BOGIE***)* You don't have to be rude.

BOGIE. I don't have to be anything. This is my park.

DAISY. *Your* park. What about that sign?

BOGIE. Just a label. You coming?

DAISY. *(reads the board)* Singles with Best Friends. 10 AM. That's now. Do we have to commit?

BOGIE. Who's we?

DAISY. Singles with Best Friends. I mean, do you date right away?

BOGIE. I don't date.

DAISY. Not you. I mean me. Or them. What do we do? *(aside to audience)*
I *know* what we do. I just don't know *when* we do it.

BOGIE. Look, lady –

DAISY. Daisy. My best friend's last dog was Lady.

BOGIE. Lady, Daisy. Like I said, just labels. I'm closing the gate.

DAISY. Wait! *(to audience)* Okay. I'll admit it, I'm rusty. I haven't played well with others for a long time. *(to* **BOGIE***)* Oh, Dog. My throat is dry. I'm panting.

BOGIE. Sit!

(**DAISY** *instantly stands alongside* **BOGIE.***)*

BOGIE. Now take a deep breath.

(**DAISY** *does as she is told.)*

DAISY. *(holding her breath, squeaks out)* Now what?

BOGIE. Breathe out.

(**DAISY** *does as she is told.)*

BOGIE. Now shake.

(**DAISY** *gives him her hand.)*

BOGIE. Good girl. *(Touches her nose.)* You feel fine.

DAISY. I'm not fine. I'm a wreck. Look my fur is coming out in clumps.

BOGIE. Stress. It can happen to any doggie.

DAISY. But it doesn't. It only happens to me. *(howls)* Why did I come here?

BOGIE. That's easy. You came to – *(reads from the sign posted on the bulletin board)* – "Meet new friends and make meaningful connections."

DAISY. So far I'm batting zero.

BOGIE. Look, Daisy. Maybe you're not cut out for the dog park scene. It ain't for cowards.

*(***BOGIE*** *starts to close gate;* ***DAISY*** *stops him.)*

DAISY. Cowards! Wait!

BOGIE. Careful. That's my gate.

DAISY. Your gate?

BOGIE. That's right.

DAISY. Your park?

BOGIE. Right again.

DAISY. *(challenges him)* This is public property. And I'm coming in.

BOGIE. *(shrugs)* That's fine. But if you're gonna play here, you're gonna play by my rules.

SONG#3: THAT'S MINE, DON'T TOUCH IT

(sings)

SEE THAT TREE

DAISY. Uh huh.

BOGIE.

SO COOL AND SHADY?
SEE THAT BENCH?

DAISY. Yes.

BOGIE.

RESERVED FOR ME?

DAISY. I said, yes.

BOGIE. *(Points to B on bark.)*

IT'S GOT MY MARK
AND SHADES THE CITY DOGPARK

*(***DAISY*** *moves to look at it.)*

BOGIE.

THAT'S MINE –
DON'T TOUCH IT.

DAISY. Who wants it?

BOGIE.

> SEE THAT BOX
> FULL OF PLAY TOYS?
> CHEWED SO HARD
> THEY LOST THEIR NOISE.
>
> YOU JUST MAY THINK
> IT'S HERE FOR EVERYBODY,
> THAT'S MINE –

DAISY. Greedy!

BOGIE.

> DON'T TOUCH IT.
>
> I'M KING OF THIS PARK,
> I RULE ALONE,
> THAT'S MY BENCH, MY BALL, MY BONE.
> I MARKED MY SPOTS SO ALL COULD SEE
> THAT EVERYTHING HERE BELONGS TO ME, ME, ME!

DAISY. Dog hog!

BOGIE. See that trash can? With the handy-bags?

DAISY. Uh-huh.

BOGIE. We pick up after ourselves around here.

DAISY. Understood.

BOGIE. That's good, 'cuz –

> *(sings)*
>
> THAT'S MINE –
> YOU CAN TOUCH IT!

DAISY. Ew!

BOGIE.

> SEE THAT HILL ,
> ALL GREEN AND GRASSY?
> WHAT A THRILL
> TO BE ON TOP!
>
> IF YOU SHOULD WANT
> TO JUMP UP HERE AND JOIN ME –
>
> *(**DAISY** makes a move toward it, **BOGIE** puts out a hand.)*
>
> DON'T EVEN THINK ABOUT IT...

BOGIE. *(cont.)*

> I CLAIMED THIS PARK SIX MONTHS AGO
> IN LATE OCTOBER BEFORE THE SNOW,
> THERE AIN'T A SPOT THAT I DON'T KNOW,
> I'M STAYING HERE UNTIL I GO, GO, GO.

DAISY. Oh, brother. I know your type. Major Control Freak. You think you're the master and I'm supposed to just rollover and play dead? Well – sit up and listen to this.

> SEE THESE EARS?
> THEY'RE HEARING BLAH-BLAH.
> SEE THIS TAIL? IT'S ON YOUR BENCH.

BOGIE. Hey!

DAISY.

> OH, LOOK I FOUND A TOY,
> IT SAYS RIGHT HERE ITS DAISY'S.

BOGIE.

> THAT'S MINE!

DAISY.

> UNH-UNH. DON'T TOUCH IT.

BOGIE. Whoa!

DAISY.

> SEE THIS HILL,
> SO GREEN AND GRASSY?
> DOES IT KILL YA
> TO SEE ME ON TOP?
> GET USED TO IT, BUB,
> CAUSE DAISY'S IN THE DOGPARK.

BOGIE. YOU'RE SASSY!

DAISY. I KNOW IT.

BOGIE.

> I'M KING OF THIS PARK

DAISY.

> SO WHERE'S YOUR THRONE?

BOGIE.

> THAT'S MY BENCH –

DAISY.

> *MY* BALL!

BOGIE.

    MY BONE!

    I MARKED MY SPOT SO ALL COULD SEE –

DAISY.

    THAT EVERYTHING HERE IS ALWAYS FREE, FREE, FREE!

DAISY.

    MY BENCH!

BOGIE.

    MY BED!

    TOUCH THAT – YOU'RE DEAD.

DAISY.

    MY STICK!

BOGIE.

    MY TREAT!

DAISY.

    MY FOOD!

    I EAT!

BOGIE.

    MY TREE, MY POOL

DAISY.

    I SWIM – YOU DROOL!

BOGIE. Wait!

    (**BOGIE** *reaches out to stop her and accidentally touches her rear.*)

DAISY.

    YOU *KNOW* THAT'S MINE!

BOGIE. Sorry.

DAISY.

    DON'T TOUCH IT!

    (**DAISY** *exits in full sassy defiance;* **BOGIE** *'s impressed.*)

BOGIE. Woof. That dame's got moxie.

    (**CHAMP** *enters in a big leap as if catching the cat toy in mid-air.*)

CHAMP. Got it! *(looks around)* Hey! Where are the girls?

BOGIE. Follow your nose! *(points offstage)*

CHAMP. I'm on the scent! *(Sees* **DAISY** *offstage.)* Whoa. She's hot.

BOGIE. So's dynamite.

*(***BOGIE*** exits behind tree;* **CHAMP** *exits and immediately returns, backing* **DAISY** *onto the stage.)*

CHAMP. Well, hello there!

DAISY. Do I know you?

CHAMP. Maybe. I'm a show dog.

DAISY. I thought you looked vaguely familiar.

CHAMP. Does this ring a bell?

*(***CHAMP*** assumes the "Air Bud" pose.)*

DAISY. Oh-my-dog. Were you Air Bud?

CHAMP. I could have been. But they wanted a retriever, not a collie. How about "It's Bacon! Bacon!"

DAISY. That was you?

CHAMP. No. But I know the Schnauzer who got it. We went to petiquette school together.

DAISY. Wow.

CHAMP. Ever use *Hartz Tick 'n' Scabies* shampoo?

DAISY. Of course not! *(to audience)* Okay, once. We had to wash everything in the house. Disgusting.

CHAMP. Remember the actor on the bottle?

(Demonstrates being in agonizing pain and scratching his ear)

DAISY. Oh Dog, yes I do!

CHAMP. *That* was me.

DAISY. Amazing. So you really are a show dog.

CHAMP. It's in my blood. I've got an audition on Monday that I'm doing some major prep for right now.

DAISY. Is it for a part in a movie?

CHAMP. Not a part. *THE* part. They want to get some footage on me for a Lassie remake. Want to go over my lines with me?

DAISY. Oh, I couldn't, I'm…I'm not a show dog.

CHAMP. With your looks you could be. Here, read this.

(**CHAMP** *walks away, doing a vocal warm-up by repeating "chew-toy" and "snausages." Assumes a dramatic pose.*)

DAISY. Okay. *(reads)* Blah blah, Lassie? *("What's wrong, Lassie?")*

CHAMP. *(drops pose, goes to* **DAISY** *like a director coaching a student)* Try it with a little more feeling. You *really* want to know what's wrong.

DAISY. *(reads with more feeling)* Blah blah, Lassie? *("What's wrong, Lassie?")*

CHAMP. Good. *(Then he acts hysterical.)* Timmy's in the well!!!!!

DAISY. Blah blah blah blah? *("What did you say?")*

CHAMP. Timmy's in the well. In the field, down by the river. *(shouts)* Can't you hear me?

DAISY. Blah blah blah blah blah, Lassie? *("Timmy's in the well, Lassie?")*

CHAMP. That's what I said. What are you, frickin' deaf? Here. I'll show you.

(**CHAMP** *circles* **DAISY** *while growling, followed by over the top dog woofs and points.*)

DAISY. Oh! Blah blah blah blah, Lassie! *("OH! Take me to him, Lassie.")*

CHAMP. That's more like it. Now, get a rope, a hammer and a ladder, and follow me.

(drops character)

Scene.

DAISY. That was really good. I'm very impressed.

CHAMP. Why thank you. You know I'm pretty impressed with you too.

DAISY. Really?

CHAMP. Yeah, with a little work, and some fur extensions – (**DAISY** *puts her paw to her neck.*) – you could be a show dog. You've got the bloodlines. I could help you.

DAISY. Oh, boy.

CHAMP. But I gotta warn you. I never do anything half way.

DAISY. I see that.

CHAMP. Last year, I played a Latin lover on the label of *Carrrne. (Rolls his "R's.")*

DAISY. *(Imitates his pronunciation.)* Carrrne?

CHAMP. Carrrne Dog Chow. Made special for the Nicaraguan marketa. Took me months to shake the accent.

DAISY. You learned an accent for a photo shoot?

CHAMP. I immerse myself in my roles. I could bring it back, like that.

(Snaps fingers.)

See? Yo soy Tangero.

SONG #4: BEST IN SHOW

CHAMP.

CAN YOU IMAGINE WHAT IT'S LIKE FOR ME
TO GAZE UPON A GIRL LIKE YOU?
MY HEART'S BURNING SO
WITH LOVE SO HOT AND OH, SO TRUE.

I CAN'T IMAGINE WHAT IT'S LIKE FOR YOU
TO BE SO CLOSE TO WHAT IS ME.
IN A BLAZE OF LIGHT
I DAZZLE ALL THAT YOU CAN SEE.

OUR PATHS WERE FATED,
OUR STARS FELL IN A PERFECT LINE.
ONCE WE'VE DATED,
TWILL BE A LOVE DIVINE.

DON'T WASTE YOUR PRECIOUS TIME ON SECOND BEST.
THE ONLY THING YOU NEED TO KNOW
IN THIS DOGPARK,
I'M THE VERY BEST IN SHOW!

(Dance break #1: CHAMP struts his stuff. DAISY comments as he dances.)

DAISY. Okay, I'm a sucker for an accent. Even if it's fake. *(Watches him dance.)* You have to admit he's got charm. *(Watches him dance some more.)* And he's pretty. *(He pulls her into an embrace.)* Pretty cocky.

CHAMP.

> DON'T EVER QUESTION WHAT YOUR HEART DESIRES,
> THE ONLY TRUTH IS WHAT YOU FEEL.
> TRY MY KISSES ON,
> THEY ARE SURE TO MAKE YOU SQUEAL.
>
> DON'T GIVE ME ICE, JUST GIVE ME DYNAMITE,
> MY HEART'S A QUARRY TO BE BLOWN.
> LIGHT MY FUSE AND SEE
> THE BIGGEST BANG YOU'VE EVER KNOWN!
>
> YOU FOXY THING, YOU MINX,
> I CAN SEE YOU LOVE THE CHASE.
> LET ME BRING TO YOU
> MY CHAMPION'S EMBRACE.
>
> YOUR LIPS SAY NO, YOUR BODY SCREAMS, YES, YES!
> STOP ACTING LIKE A SILLY CHILD.
> DO YOU HEAR THAT CRY?
> IT'S THE CALLING OF THE WILD!

(Dance break #2: **CHAMP** *pulls* **DAISY** *into sexy latin dance)*

DAISY. Look at me, I'm dancing with a dog with no brain! *(more dancing)* And I love it! Ay-yi-yi!

CHAMP.

> AND NOW THAT YOU HAVE DANCED WITH ME,
> YOU SEE THE BEAUTY IN THIS BEAST.
> IT'S TIME TO TAKE THE PLUNGE
> INTO MY LOVE'S DELICIOUS FEAST.
>
> LOOK AT US, WE MAKE THE PERFECT PAIR,
> LIKE STARS ABOVE WE CAST A GLOW.
> AND ALL THE WORLD CAN SEE
> THAT WE –
> THAT'S YOU AND ME –
> WERE MEANT TO BE
> THE BEST IN SHOW!

(‌**CHAMP** *freezes in final dance pose, holding* **DAISY** *in a drop position.)*

(SFX: Offstage voice: "Yo! Champ. Here boy!")

CHAMP. *(drops* **DAISY***)* Sorry, Lola. My Best Friend Forever calls.

DAISY. Daisy.

CHAMP. Huh?

DAISY. My name's Daisy.

CHAMP. Right. Daily. *(turns and yells offstage)* Coming, pal!

    *(***CHAMP*** exits.* **DAISY** *shaken up but thrilled…)*

DAISY. *(to audience)* Ruff. He's one hot dog.

BOGIE. *(Appears from around the side of the tree.)* You're not the first to say that.

DAISY. Where'd you come from?

BOGIE. My tree.

DAISY. Now let's not start *that* again.

BOGIE. Deal. Couldn't help watching you. Nice moves. You've done this before.

DAISY. Never in *this* park. You?

BOGIE. I don't get involved with that hooey. I'm a lone dog. The only member of my pack.

DAISY. What about your BFF?

BOGIE. Huh? Ah, he's no joiner either.

DAISY. I thought I wasn't, but I'm starting to think differently.

BOGIE. Because of Champ? Careful. He's handsome, I'll give you that. But dig a little deeper and you'll discover – well, he's handsome.

DAISY. Jealous?

BOGIE. Nah, never much interested in outward beauty. Though I can certainly appreciate it when I see it, present company included.

DAISY. *(surprised)* Why, that was a compliment!

BOGIE. I call 'em as I see em.

DAISY. *(to audience)* He's not such a jerk after all.

    (SFX: PA ANNOUNCER: "Agility class will convene on the green in two minutes.")

DAISY. My BFF signed me up for that. You going? It's collars optional.

BOGIE. What are you talking about?

DAISY. I noticed you're not wearing a collar.

BOGIE. *(shrugs)* Just another label.

(SFX: Work-out music in BG, PA announces: "All hounds on deck to make it burn.")

(SFX: Whistle)

BOGIE. That's my cue. Chow, Daisy. *(Disappears behind tree.)*

DAISY. *(to audience)* This park is starting to get interesting.

*(**ITCHY** runs up, out of breath, tries to hide behind **DAISY**)*

ITCHY. Hide me!

DAISY. Hold it, hold it, Tiger. I don't even know you.

ITCHY. Name's Itchy.

DAISY. What's going on?

ITCHY. Agility class. Can't do it. I got…I got… *(sneezes)* Shitzu!

DAISY. Dachsundheit.

ITCHY. Sniffulus. I brought a note from my best friend. See? I got sniffulus. *(shows piece of paper)*

DAISY. That's your handwriting.

ITCHY. How can you tell?

DAISY. *(holds up paper, revealing paw prints)* It's got your paws all over it.

ITCHY. So you caught me. I always get caught. Why is that? Other guys get away with everything. Chewing the couch, the shoes, getting in the garbage. I always get caught.

DAISY. Maybe you should try not doing it.

ITCHY. I try. I *try!* I can't help myself. It's my nerves. The doc says I'm humperactive.

DAISY. Really. *(Steps back.)*

ITCHY. Don't worry. I got a handle on that. I chew my paw, instead. See? I've got a hole right there.

DAISY. Ew! I used to scratch my fur out right at the collar, every time my BFF left me alone.

ITCHY. That sounds like flea-bitis. I had that once.

DAISY. Me too. Thank Dog it went away.

ITCHY. I had that thing where I couldn't walk across linoleum.

DAISY. Floor-ide?

ITCHY. Yeah.

DAISY. I'm afraid of thunder, gunshots –

ITCHY. Doorbells, sirens –

DAISY. Vacuum cleaners, wind-up toys – did I mention vacuum cleaners?

ITCHY. I got one word for you – Fourth of July.

DAISY. Ahhhh! *(covers ears)* I'm not listening.

> **(ITCHY** *does fireworks sounds with piccolo petes and explosions depicting in seconds the entire Fourth of July with* Stars and Stripes Forever.*)*

DAISY. You're funny. *(Lowers hands, speaks to audience.)* He's funny. *(Looks at* **ITCHY***, and back at audience.)* In a neurotic, twitchy sort of way.

> *(to* **ITCHY***)*

> I know a book you should read. It's called "How to Be Your Own Best Friend."

ITCHY. Read it.

DAISY. The paw print edition?

ITCHY. Yep, it's completely dog-eared.

> *(SFX: Announcer: "This is it. Time to get fit!")*

ITCHY. Panic! Pulse rate going up! And up! Stomach cramp. Code Red! *(Grabs a handful of grass and shoves it in his mouth.)* Gonna blow!

DAISY. Calm down. You can do this.

ITCHY. I can't. I'll be the laughing stock. I have short legs and a stubby tail and a high bark.

DAISY. Of course you do. You're a Jack Russell.

ITCHY. Girls always make fun of me. Even my mother.

DAISY. No!

ITCHY. Yes!

SONG #5: ITCHY'S LAMENT

ITCHY.
WHEN I WAS JUST YOUNG PUP,
NO BEAUTY TO MY MOTHER,
SHE TOOK A SECOND LOOK, SAID, "SON,
YOU'LL NEVER BE A LOVER."
AND AT THAT MOMENT I JUST KNEW
WHAT WOULD BECOME MY FATE.
I'D BE THE DOG THAT OTHER DOGS
WOULD BITE AND KICK AND HATE.

DAISY. That's so sad.

ITCHY. Try tragic!
AND WHEN I LEFT THE LITTER
AND SET OUT ON MY OWN,
THE OTHER DOGS WOULD AMBUSH ME
AND RUN OFF WITH MY BONE.
IT GOT SO BAD THAT I WOULD PEE
THE MOMENT THEY DREW NEAR,
AND ANYONE THAT CAME AT ME
SAW MY RETREATING REAR.

AND OH, THE THINGS THEY SAID!
OH, THEY RUN AROUND MY HEAD!

HEY STUBBY, TUBBY, MAMA'S BOY,
SHRIMPY WIMPY MUTT!
AH! GET LOST,
GO BITE YOURSELF ,
AND CHASE YOUR BLUBBER BUTT!
PISSY, SISSY, CREEPY PUP,
STAY HERE YOU'LL GET LICKED!
IN SPORTS, YOU'RE JUST A BOOGER,
THE LAST ONE TO BE PICKED.

DAISY. That must have been hard.

ITCHY. You don't know the half of it.
AND THEN I WAS ADOPTED,

A PENTHOUSE WAS MY HOME
BUT MY BEST FRIEND LEFT AT 8
AND I WAS ALL ALONE.
I DROOLED, I HOWLED, I PANICKED,
THEN I FOUND THE SHOES.
AND SO IN DESPERATION
I CHEWED AWAY MY BLUES.

AND OH, THE THINGS HE SAID
OH, THEY RUN AROUND MY HEAD!

BAD DOG, BAD DOG, YOU'RE THE WORST
GET AWAY FROM ME, GO FETCH!
I MEAN IT, DOWN! GET OFF THE COUCH
YOUR BREATH, IT MAKES ME RETCH
DON'T LICK THAT! OH GOD, THAT'S GROSS!
THIS DOG IS GETTING FAT.
WHAT HAVE YOU BEEN ROLLING IN?
I SHOULD HAVE BOUGHT A CAT!

DAISY. You were a puppy. I'm sure things are better now.

ITCHY. Worse?

NOW OLDER BUT NO WISER,
I PACE THE FLOOR AT NIGHT.
I WORRY, ARE MY JOKES TOO BAD?
DO GIRLS THINK I'M UPTIGHT?
I LIE THERE IN THE DARKNESS
AND TRY TO GO TO SLEEP,
AND COUNT MY FEARS AND FAILURES
INSTEAD OF COUNTING SHEEP.

AND OH, THE THOUGHTS I THINK!
OH! THEY PUSH ME TO THE BRINK!

I THINK MY HAIR'S RECEDING,
I KNOW I'M A-D-D.
MY COLLAR MAKES MY BUTT LOOK BIG,
CAN CANINES GET E-D?
I EAT FROM THE CATBOX,
SOME MIGHT THINK THAT'S CRASS,
I HAVE A FEAR OF SWEATING,
THAT'S WHY I CAN'T TAKE THIS CLASS!

(**ITCHY** *runs off stage, as* **TRIX** *[a poodle played by* **CHAMP**] *and* **GINGER** *[an Afghan played by* **BOGIE**] *enter.*)

TRIX (CHAMP). Woo! Look at that dog run! Ears back and tail between his legs.

GINGER (BOGIE). Well, he better get his furry butt back here. I'm not in this for my health. *(Starts to go after him.)* Wait. Trix? Do I have dogbreath?

TRIX (CHAMP). Whoo-wee. You sure do, Ginger.

GINGER. Good. Here Bowzer. Come to Mama. *(Exits.)*

TRIX (CHAMP). Since when did we become the Girl Scouts? Where are the guys?

DAISY. I'm glad they aren't here. Those hounds want only one thing.

TRIX (CHAMP). To roll in poop and eat their own barf.

DAISY. Ah, that's not what I was thinking, but yes.

TRIX (CHAMP). Now, don't get me wrong, I like dirty dogs. But if they're too busy making their mark and not looking at me, then I say –

DAISY. Go chase a parked car.

TRIX. You said it, sister. Hmmm. Looks like Bogie's been here today. *(Reads the signs on tree, box, trash can and fire hydrant like they're visible.)* Me. Me. Mine. Mine. Paws off. That is one dog who owns his territory.

DAISY. Don't I know it.

TRIX. Can I give you a little tip?

DAISY. I guess.

TRIX. Watch out for Sheila, she's a herder. Always trying to get us to circle up and do what she wants to do.

DAISY. I'll be careful.

(**GINGER** *[***BOGIE***] enters carrying* **ITCHY**, *who now sports a headband.*)

ITCHY. No please no!

DAISY. Itchy!

GINGER (BOGIE). Caught him trying to dig his way out under the fence. *(Puts* **ITCHY** *down.)* Heel, puppy.

ITCHY. I'm a one-on-one personal trainer kind of canine. You girls… I'm just outta my league.

TRIX (CHAMP). I'll say. Grow a pair and follow me.

SONG #6: HOT DOGS

ALL.

> HEADS UP HIGH! OUR CLOCKS ARE TICKING
> AND IT MAKES US CRY.
> TAILS UP HIGH! WE FEEL THE BURNING HEAT
> AND I'LL TELL YOU WHY.
>
> WE'RE ON THE HUNT FOR A DOG, A CUR
> WHO LIKES TO CUDDLE WITH A GIRL IN FUR
> WE'RE ON THE SCENT FOR A MR. RIGHT
> WHO'LL HOLD US THROUGH THE NIGHT

GINGER (BOGIE).

> HE GOES SNIFF, I PLAY DISCREET,
> HE'S A BRUTE WHO'S FIRM BUT SWEET.
> STRUTS HIS STUFF, IT AIN'T RIGHT,
> I TURN TAIL AND SAY GOOD NIGHT.

TRIX. Adios, puppy.

GINGER (BOGIE). Ciao! Baby

ITCHY. Call me?

DAISY. Don't act so needy

ITCHY. What should I do?

DAISY. Show 'em what ya got!

ITCHY. Watch this, girls!

> **(ITCHY** *tries to lift the exercise equipment, can't budge it.* **TRIX** *and* **GINGER** *pick it up without effort and continue song.)*

ALL.

> HEADS UP HIGH! OUR CLOCKS ARE TICKING
> AND IT MAKES US CRY.
> TAILS UP HIGH! WE FEEL THE BURNING HEAT
> AND I'LL TELL YOU WHY.

> WE'RE ON THE HUNT FOR A DOG, A CUR,
> WHO LIKES TO CUDDLE WITH A GIRL IN FUR.
> WE'RE ON THE TRAIL OF A BREED THAT'S PURE
> WHO WANTS A GODDESS AND THINKS I'M HER.

TRIX (CHAMP).

> HE COMES UP, HIS HEAD IS LOW,
> SAYS WITH A GROWL, "COME ON, LET'S GO."
> CHECK HIM OUT, HE FAILS THE TEST,
> SAY BYE-BYE CAUSE I WANT THE BEST.

TRIX (CHAMP). Down, boy!

GINGER (BOGIE). Heel, Bowzer!

DAISY. I think Ginger likes you.

ITCHY. You think so?

DAISY. Look at the way she's dancing for you.

ITCHY. That's a lotta girl.

DAISY.

> HE WANTS MY BODY BUT LOVES MY MIND,
> FACE TO FACE, HE'S OH SO FINE.
> I SAY I CARE, IF HE WON'T BITE
> I'M ALL HIS FROM MORN TIL NIGHT.

GINGER (BOGIE). Where is that Prince Charming?

DAISY. He's out there, I know it.

TRIX (CHAMP). Here, Prince! Come on, boy!

DAISY. You're turn, Itchy. Tell us how you feel.

ITCHY. *(with full bravado)* This is it, the time is now, the Itch Machine's gonna show ya how!

> *(sings)*

> HEADS UP HIGH, TODAY I'M LUCKY.
> AND I JUST CAN'T LIE.
> TAILS UP HIGH, I'M FEELING FRISKY,
> AND I'LL TELL YOU WHY.

ITCHY. *(cont.)*

> I'M ON THE SCENT OF A PUP PLAYMATE
> WHO THINKS THAT I'M THE BEST DARN DATE.
> I'M ON THE MAKE FOR A FULL-SIZED QUEEN
> WHO'S LOOKING FOR LEAN AND MEAN.

> I DON'T CARE IF SHE'S LOST A TAIL,
> HER EARS ARE CROPPED AND ONE EYE'S PALE,
> CRUSTY SCABS ALL OVER HER HEAD,
> COME ON, MAMA, JUMP IN BED!

DAISY. Itchy!

ITCHY. Follow me, Girls! Let's get those tails a-waggin' and feel the burn. We're dogs in heat!

TRIX. Right behind ya.

ITCHY. Let's get those tails waggin' and make it burn, we're dog's in heat.

*(**ITCHY** leads the "girls" in a pole dance break.)*

> Weave. Weave. Weave. Weave.
> Mount your pole, rock and roll.
> Shake it off. Good dog.
> And bump… And bump…
> And grind…
> Say what? *(head cock)* Oh.
> Say what? *(head cock)* Oh!
> And search and rescue
> And search and rescue.
> Over here *(they point)*.
> Cookie?
> Make your mark.
> This is my dog park.

TRIX. Itchy!

GINGER. You ain't nothing but a hound dog!

DAISY. My dogs are barking!

ALL.

> FEEL THE HEAT! WE'RE BURNING BOOTY
> AND WE'RE SWEATING SWEET.
> CAN'T COOL DOWN! WE'VE GOT HIM
> HOT ON THE GRIDDLE!

DAISY.

> WITH A SIZZLE IN THE MIDDLE!

ITCHY.

> I'M A HUNKA HOUND!

ALL.

> HOT DOGS!

> (**ITCHY** *rides off on* **GINGER***'s back.* **TRIX** *follows them offstage.*)

GINGER (BOGIE). Whoo! I'm in puppy love!

ITCHY. Ride em, 'cowboy!

TRIX (CHAMP). Wait for me, saddlebags!

> (*SFX [Stage Left]:* **GINGER** *and* **TRIX** *howling and yelling,* **ITCHY** *calling back to* **DAISY**.)

DAISY. *(calls after* **ITCHY***)* Way to go, Itchy! You got what you wanted. Two Great Dames with big… paws. Why is it so hard to find what I want?

> (*SFX [Stage Right]: MORE DOGS PLAYING. "Give me the ball" "Go long"*)

DAISY. *(turns to audience)* I know I can be a little weepy. But only when I'm alone. Which is most of the time. Well, who wouldn't cry? Is it so wrong to want a friend?

SONG#7: SOMEONE, SOMEWHERE, SOMEDAY (DAISY)

DAISY.

> SOMEWHERE
> I HOPE THAT THERE WILL BE
> THE PERFECT ONE FOR ME,
> SOMEDAY I KNOW I'LL SEE

> SOMEONE
> WHO'S FUNNY KIND AND FAIR,
> SOMEONE WHO'LL ALWAYS CARE,
> WHOSE LOVE WILL SURELY GROW,
> I KNOW

> HE'S THERE,
> AND SOMEDAY SOON
> I'LL TURN AROUND AND SEE
> THAT PERFECT SOMEONE
> LOOKING BACK
> AT ME.

(During the song **BOGIE** *steps from behind his tree and leans on it, watching and listening.)*

BOGIE. *(to audience)* What did I tell ya? Trouble with a capital T.

DAISY. *(notices* **BOGIE***)* Oh! I didn't see you. How long have you been there?

BOGIE. Long enough.

DAISY. Well…now you know. *(Starts scratching at her neck.)*

BOGIE. Whoa, whoa. Careful there. You'll give yourself collara.

DAISY. Collara?

BOGIE. It's a nervous condition. Where your fur falls out. Right at the collar.

DAISY. *(looking at his lack of collar)* I guess you don't have that problem.

BOGIE. Yeah, I'm one of the lucky ones.

(SFX: "Call to the Hunt" racetrack music)

(SFX: PA Announcer: "Speed Mating will begin in 3 minutes. All bachelors and bachelorettes, meet at the K-9 clubhouse in 3 minutes.")

DAISY. You going?

BOGIE. Not my style.

DAISY. Scared you might meet someone you like?

BOGIE. I've already done that.

DAISY. *(to audience)* Smooth. *(back to* **BOGIE***)* Come to the clubhouse. It should be fun.

BOGIE. *(shaking head)* I don't know. …

DAISY. Come on!

BOGIE. It's just not my –

DAISY. Please? For me?

BOGIE. *(goes along)* I oughta have my head examined.

SONG #8: GOTTA PICK ME

*(***CHAMP** *and* **ITCHY** *bring on dog headbands and pass them out among the dogs or they can bring on K9 Clubhouse with windows á la Laugh In.)*

ALL.

> GOTTA PICK ME!
> GOTTA PICK ME!
> GOTTA PICK ME!
> GOTTA PICK ME NOW!
>
> *(SFX: PA VOICE: "You have 1 minute to meet your mate, take a whiff and make a date.")*

ALL.

> GOTTA PICK ME!
> GOTTA PICK ME!
> GOTTA PICK ME!
> GOTTA PICK ME NOW!
>
> *(SFX: BUZZER)*
>
> *(SFX: PA VOICE: "Hear the buzzer? That's your cue. Time to move on to someone new.")*

BOGIE.

> JUST A MINUTE TO TELL YOUR TALE,
> GOTTA BE SMART AND FUN.

DAISY.

> NOT ENOUGH TIME TO MAKE A SALE
> AND BE THE CHOSEN ONE.

ALL.

> GOTTA PICK ME!
> GOTTA PICK ME!
> GOTTA PICK ME!
> GOTTA PICK ME NOW!
>
> (**ITCHY** *and* **BOGIE** *in Window 1*)

SKANK THE CHINESE CRESTED CHIHUAHUA (ITCHY).

> I'm part-Schlepard, part Siberian Hussy. And all yours.

ALL.

> GOTTA PICK ME!
> GOTTA PICK ME!
> GOTTA PICK ME!
> GOTTA PICK ME NOW!

(**CHAMP** *as* **BRUTUS** – *he has an eye-patch, tattoo of a skull, and scars and barely any hair and* **DAISY** *in Window 2.*)

BRUTUS (CHAMP). The trouble with obedience school is you learn all this stuff you'll never use in the real world.

ALL.
GOTTA PICK ME!
GOTTA PICK ME!
GOTTA PICK ME!
GOTTA PICK ME NOW!

(**SKANK** *[***ITCHY***] in Window 1 and* **BRUTUS** *[***CHAMP***] in Window 2.*)

SKANK (ITCHY). Whatever you rolled in sure smells great!

BRUTUS (CHAMP). Back atcha.

SKANK (ITCHY).
THAT FIRST IMPRESSION MAY BE YOUR LAST
SO TRY HARD NOT TO BEG.

BRUTUS (CHAMP).
TELL THEM NOTHING ABOUT YOUR PAST
AND PLEASE, STAY OFF HER LEG.

ALL.
GOTTA PICK ME!
GOTTA PICK ME!
GOTTA PICK ME!
GOTTA PICK ME NOW!

(**DAISY** *as the* **DEPRESSED DOWNER BASSETT** *in window 3 and* **SKANK** *[***ITCHY***] in window 2.*)

DOWNER BASSETT (DAISY). I have hair in weird places.

SKANK (ITCHY). Tell me about it.

ALL.
GOTTA PICK ME!
GOTTA PICK ME!
GOTTA PICK ME!
GOTTA PICK ME NOW!

(**BOGIE** *as an* **ENGLISH SHEEPDOG** *in window 1 is joined by* **DOWNER** *[*DAISY*].*)

ENGLISH SHEEPDOG (BOGIE). If you ask me, I think animal testing is a terrible idea.

DOWNER BASSETT (DAISY). Yeah, I get all nervous and give the wrong answers.

ALL.

> GOTTA PICK ME!
> GOTTA PICK ME!
> GOTTA PICK ME!
> GOTTA PICK ME NOW!

ENGLISH SHEEPDOG (BOGIE). *(in window 2)*

> I'll admit, on occasion, I enjoy a drink from the toilet bowl. Who doesn't?

> *(sings)*

> YOU MIGHT FIND A DIAMOND HERE,
> OR A LUMP OF COAL,
> BUT THIS IS SUCH A SWINGIN' PLACE,
> WHO CARES? LET'S ROCK AND ROLL!

ALL.

> GOTTA PICK ME!
> GOTTA PICK ME!
> GOTTA PICK ME!
> GOTTA PICK ME NOW!

> (**CHAMP** *at window 1 with* **DAISY**)

CHAMP. I spend half my life at the groomer, half at the gym, and the other half on the phone with my agent. You do the math.

ALL.

> GOTTA PICK ME!
> GOTTA PICK ME!
> GOTTA PICK ME!
> GOTTA PICK ME NOW!

ITCHY. *(by himself in window 2 calling out to girl who's left)*

> Hey, Did I mention I do balloon animals? Wait, come back.

ALL.

> GOTTA PICK ME!
> GOTTA PICK ME!
> GOTTA PICK ME!
> GOTTA PICK ME NOW!

> *(**BOGIE** and **DAISY** in window 1.)*

DAISY. See, Bogie? This is fun and it's free.

BOGIE. Yeah, there's always free cheese in a mousetrap.

BOGIE.

> THERE'S JUST SOMETHING ABOUT YOU
> MAKES ME WEAK IN THE KNEES.

DAISY.

> THIS MIGHT BE SOMETHING SPECIAL,
> WHY NOT STICK AROUND AND SEE?

ALL.

> GOTTA PICK ME, GOTTA PICK ME!
> GOTTA PICK ME, GOTTA PICK ME!
> GOTTA PICK ME,
> GOTTA GOTTA PICK ME,
> GOTTA GOTTA GOTTA PICK ME –
> RIGHT NOW!

> *(SFX: BUZZER)*

> *(SFX: PA Voice: "Grab your pup, the time is up!")*

> *(**ITCHY** and **CHAMP** push K-9 Clubhouse off, revealing **DAISY** and **BOGIE** behind it. **CHAMP** pauses to talk to **DAISY**.)*

CHAMP. Lovers with Leashes is next. The main event. We leave the park and go for twilight bark. How about it, Daily?

DAISY. It's Daisy.

CHAMP. Yeah, Daisy. Right. You and me?

DAISY. Um, Champ, give me a minute, will you?

CHAMP. Sure thing, Maisy. I'll try to let the other girls down easy.

DAISY. You do that.

(**ITCHY** *runs back on, out of breath.*)

ITCHY. Daisy, will you be my partner?

DAISY. What about Ginger or Trix?

ITCHY. They ran off with the Beagle Brothers. Besides, you're the one I really wanted to –

DAISY. Itchy, hold on, will you? I was just talking to Bogie here.

ITCHY. Sure thing. Sorry, Bogie. No harm meant.

BOGIE. None taken.

(**ITCHY** *starts to sit on the bench.*)

BOGIE. Ah, ah, ah!

(**ITCHY** *stops in mid-sit.*)

ITCHY. Your bench. I got the message. Whoa! What's this?

BOGIE. *(turns back to* **DAISY***)* You were saying?

(**ITCHY** *finds jacket and ties it around his shoulders like a cape. Climbs on bench, pretends to fly.*)

ITCHY. Look at me, "There's no need to fear. Underdog is here!"

BOGIE. Hey! Give me that! *(grabs jacket)* This is private property!

ITCHY. Sorry, Boge. I was just joking. Ha-ha-ha? A joke?

BOGIE. Do I look like I'm laughing?

DAISY. Bogie, calm down.

BOGIE. Where's your brain, you little pipsqueak.

ITCHY. I don't know, Boge. I wasn't thinking.

BOGIE. You never think. Now beat it, will ya?

DAISY. Bogie!

ITCHY. I was waiting to talk to Daisy.

BOGIE. Yeah, well you're barking up the wrong tree. Now scram.

ITCHY. Daisy's your girl? Is that what you mean?

DAISY. *(surprised)* Is that what you mean?

BOGIE. I don't mean anything I'll admit. Now get outta here.

ITCHY. I'm going. I'm going.

DAISY. Sorry, Itchy. See ya later.

ITCHY. *(feelings hurt)* I doubt it. *(mutters)* Son of a bitch…

 (**ITCHY** *exits.*)

BOGIE. *(after an uncomfortable silence)* Sorry about that. I don't like guys touching my stuff.

 (Pause as he folds up and stashes his jacket.)

DAISY. Really? I hadn't noticed.

BOGIE. Shouldn't a flown off the handle like that. I like Itch.

DAISY. Ya sure have a funny way of showing it. Why don't you count to 10?

BOGIE. Why don't I go to China? Some things you do and some things you don't.

DAISY. What's your story, Bogie?

BOGIE. Which story do you want? The funny one or the heartbreaker?

DAISY. Which one do you want to tell?

BOGIE. One leads to the other.

DAISY. Ever been in love?

BOGIE. Sure. Lots of times. You?

DAISY. Oh, don't get me started.

BOGIE. Go ahead. I ain't going anywhere.

SONG #9: LOOKING FOR LOVE

DAISY.

 I'VE LOOKED FOR LOVE IN ALL THE WRONG FACES,
 SEARCHING SMILES FOR THE SLIGHTEST TRACES THAT HE'LL

DAISY. *(cont.)*

 BE THE LOVE THAT'S REAL.
 GUESS I WAS DREAMIN'.

 IF I HADN'T SEEN HOW EACH NEW LOVE FADED,
 THEN I MIGHT BE EASILY PERSUADED TO
 FALL IN LOVE ANEW,
 WHAT CAN I DO?

OH, I KNOW,
I SHOULDN'T BRING MYSELF MORE SORROW,
WHY WEAR MY HEART UPON MY SLEEVE?
YET INSIDE
I DREAM EACH NEW TOMORROW
WILL BRING THAT KISS
THAT GIVES ME BLISS.

SO I STILL LOOK IN ALL THE WRONG FACES,
HOPING TO FIND MY ONE AND ONLY EMBRACEABLE YOU
WHO'LL NEVER MAKE ME BLUE,
WHO WON'T LOVE ME AND LEAVE ME,
WON'T HURT OR DECEIVE ME,
THAT WONDERFUL ONE
WHO'LL MAKE MY DREAMS COME TRUE.

DAISY. So, Lovers with Leashes. How about it?

BOGIE. You extending an invite? To me?

DAISY. Yes. *(voice husky with possibility)* So, what do you say?

BOGIE. I can't.

DAISY. What?

BOGIE. I can't leave.

DAISY. You already have a date?

BOGIE. *(shakes his head)* I, uh… I made a promise.

DAISY. *(major embarrassment)* Oh, my dog. I totally misread…
everything – I'm so embarrassed. This is just so…Is my
nose hot? It feels hot. Oh, Dog.

BOGIE. Listen, Daisy, you got it all wrong –

DAISY. I'll say. I went out on a limb, and it broke. That'll
teach me.

BOGIE. No, no –

DAISY. Don't try to spare my feelings. I'm an idiot.

(**DAISY** *runs out the gate.*)

BOGIE. Daisy! Wait!

DAISY. *(to audience) (head in paws)* Someone, please, put me
out of my misery!

SONG # 10 EVERY DOG MUST HAVE HER DAY

(Opening chords of song make **DAISY** *lift her head.* **PURSE DOGS** *[hand puppets operated by actors playing* **BOGIE** *and* **ITCHY***] appear stage right.)*

PURSE DOGS.

> BOW WOW WOW-DE-OW!
> BOW WOW WOW-DE-OW!
> BOW BUBBA DABOW BUBBADBOW
> YIP! ARF! WOOF!
> DON'T QUIT NOW, YOU'RE ON THE SCENT,
> GOOD THINGS WILL COME YOUR WAY.
> STAY WITH THE PACK,
> YOU'RE ON THE RIGHT TRACK
> EVERY DOG MUST HAVE HER DAY!
> JUST IGNORE THAT SILLY MUTT,
> HIS BARK'S WORSE THAN HIS BITE.
> YOU CAN GROWL OR EVEN HOWL,
> BUT DON'T GIVE UP WITHOUT A FIGHT.

DAISY.

> SO TELL ME WHY SHOULD I
> EVEN TRY TO PLAY THIS LAME OLD GAME?
> IT'S SUCH A CHORE,
> HE'S A BORE,
> I'VE DONE IT BEFORE
> AND I WANT MORE!

PURSE DOGS.

> HEY, MISS DAISY, LIGHTEN UP,
> A RAINBOW'S ON ITS WAY!
> PUT ON A SMILE, AND AFTER A WHILE
> YOU'LL SEE THIS DOG,
> WE MEAN THIS DOG,
> THAT'S RIGHT, EVERY DOG
> MUST HAVE HER DAY!
> OOOH!

DAISY. *(to* **PURSE DOGS***)* Thanks, I needed that.

CHAMP. *(runs onstage)* Daisy! Lovers with Leashes is leaving the building.

DAISY. I… I…

CHAMP. He who hesitates is sometimes – uh…

BOGIE. *(appears from behind tree)* Lost.

CHAMP. *(sticks head out from stage right)* Exactly. So let's get on the love bus and ride.

DAISY. But what about Itchy…

CHAMP. Don't worry about the Itch-dawg. He's with that Siberian Hussy. *(lowers voice)* Everybody's been with her. But hey, I'm not telling. *(normal voice)* So, it's lovers, my specialty, with leashes. Are you with me?

DAISY. *(with a look back at* **BOGIE***)* Well, sure. Why not? You big hunk of Carrrne. You lead and I'll follow, El Tangero.

CHAMP. Con mucho gusto!

DAISY. *(to* **BOGIE***)* Adios, Perrrrrrro!

(Both exit yelling "Ay Ay Yi!" and "Arf Arf" Latin dance squeals of delight.)

BOGIE. Of all the dog parks, in all the cities, in all the world, she had to walk into mine. Damn!

(It's sunset at the dog park. **BOGIE** *sits on top of the toy box and looks out at the city.)*

I gotta stay. I made a promise and I'm sticking with it.

SONG #11: SOMEONE, SOMEWHERE, SOMEDAY (BOGIE)

BOGIE.

SOMEWHERE
I KNOW THERE'S GONNA BE
A HAPPY END FOR ME
SOMEDAY I'M GONNA SEE

BOGIE. *(cont.)*

SOMEONE
WHOSE WHISTLE CALLS ME HOME
NO MATTER WHERE WE ROAM
WE'LL NEVER BE ALONE.
YES

I BELIEVE
THAT SOMEDAY SOON
I'LL TURN AROUND AND SEE
MY FAITHFUL FRIEND
COMING BACK
FOR ME.

Goodnight, pal.

End of Act One

ACT TWO

*(Lights up on **CHAMP** in a cone, **ITCHY** in a bumblebee costume, and **BOGIE** tied to the fire hydrant. They are howling in the dark.)*

SONG #12: DEEP DOG DOO WOP

ALL.

> DEEP DOG DOO WOP
> DEEP DOG DOO WOP

CHAMP. He told me I was getting "tutored."

ALL.

> DEEP DOG DOO WOP

ITCHY. He said we were going to a costume party.

ALL.

> DEEP DOG DOO WOP

BOGIE. Somebody snitched. Now I'm going up river.

ALL.

> DEEP DOG DEEP DEEP DOG DOO WOP!

CHAMP.

> WANNA SEE A SORE LOSER?
> TAKE A GOOD LOOK AT ME.
> 'CAUSE I WENT AND TRUSTED MY FRIEND,
> MY CAREER'S AT AN END
> NO MORE LOVERS FOR ME, NO MORE LEADS.
> AND I DON'T KNOW
> IF I'M A HE OR A SHE,
> OH, I'M IN –

ALL.

> DEEP DOG DOO WOP
> DEEP DOG DOO WOP

ITCHY.

> WANNA SEE A JOKE IN BLACK STRIPES?
> THAT WOULD HAVE TO BE ME.
> NO WONDER THE GIRLS RUN AWAY
> WHEN I ASK THEM TO PLAY
> WHO'D BE SEEN WITH AN INSECT LIKE ME?
> THAT'S WHY I SNAPPED
> AND BIT THE HAND THAT DID THIS TO ME
> NOW I'M IN –

ALL.

> DEEP DOG DOO WOP
> DEEP DOG DOO WOP

BOGIE.

> IF YOU WANNA SEE STUPID
> TAKE A GANDER AT ME
> 'CAUSE I MADE THE BIGGEST MISTAKE
> A DUMB MUTT CAN MAKE
> I LET SOME DOLL GET TOO CLOSE TO ME
> HOW COULD I KNOW
> SHE'D GO AND BLOW THE WHISTLE ON ME?
> NOW I'M IN –

ALL.

> DEEP DOG DOO WOP
> DEEP DOG DOO WOP
>
> WHO-OO-OO BLEW THE WHISTLE?
> WHO-OO-OO CALLED THE VET?
> WHO-OO-OO PICKED THIS COSTUME?
> WELL, HERE ARE THEIR NAMES
> FROM THE GREAT WALL OF SHAME:

ITCHY.

> MY BEST FRIEND.

CHAMP.

> MY AGENT.

BOGIE.

> THAT DAME.

ALL.

> DEEP DOG DOO WOP
>
> (**BOGIE** *catches his neck on rope: UNH-UNH-UNH*)
>
> DEEP DOG DOO WOP
>
> (**CHAMP** *pulls his stitches: OW-OW-OW*)
>
> DEEP DOG DOO WOP
>
> (**ITCHY** *tries to bite off his insect wings: ARGH-ARGH-ARGH*)
>
> DEEP DOG DOO WOP...

DAISY. *(offstage)* You tricked me. You said we were going for a Peticure. This isn't Paws and Claws.

ITCHY. It's Daisy. Hide!

BOGIE. Back here.

> (*All three bolt for the tree, but* **CHAMP** *can't get behind it because his cone keeps getting caught on the tree.*)

DAISY. *(offstage)* OOOOOO! I could just bite you!

CHAMP. Ow! Ow. Ow.

DAISY. *(Sees* **CHAMP***)* Champ!

CHAMP. *(acting casual against the garbage can)* Why, hello there.

DAISY. What happened to you?

CHAMP. Hmm?

DAISY. The cone.

CHAMP. Oh, that. Well….

ITCHY. He was NEUT –

CHAMP. *(silences* **ITCHY***)* I was NEW… to the, uh, set for the Carrrrne Lite Dog Chow shoot and I, uh, tripped over some cables and hurt myself.

DAISY. Did you get stitches?

CHAMP. I'm not sure.

> (**CHAMP** *bends over and* **ITCHY***, who is still hiding, checks out his butt.*)

ITCHY. It looks like at least 20.

CHAMP. *(shocked)* 20!

DAISY. Where?

CHAMP. That's personal. My Dog! You fans are all alike. An actor can't go for a walk or out to eat without being hounded –

DAISY. Fans? I'm not a fan. I'm a show dog. You said so.

CHAMP. Don't flatter yourself.

(**CHAMP** *exits, walking gingerly.*)

DAISY. What got into him?

ITCHY. *(Appears from behind tree.)* A surgical knife.

DAISY. You don't mean....

ITCHY. You didn't hear it from me. And quit staring, will you?

DAISY. I was just wondering about the stripes and the antennae?

ITCHY. Stop wondering and don't look at me. Better yet, don't even talk to me.

DAISY. Itchy! What did I do?

ITCHY. I mean it. I want to be alone.

DAISY. Well, if that's how you feel, why don't you just fly away!

ITCHY. I knew it! You just got here and already you're starting with the bumblebee jokes.

DAISY. Well, what's with the get-up?

ITCHY. Mind your own –

DAISY. Beeswax?

ITCHY. See? You and your whole sex. Cold, cruel, castrating – *(sneezes)* Shitzu.

DAISY. Dachseunheit. Your sniffulus is acting up again.

ITCHY. There you go. Making fun of the little guy. I don't have to sit here and take this.

(**ITCHY** *exits.*)

DAISY. Then – buzz off!

(**DAISY** *paws floor in exasperation, then sits on bench as* **PURSE DOGS** *appear from behind tree.*)

SONG #13: WRONG DOG

PURSE DOGS.

WHY ARE YOU ALWAYS PICKING THE WRONG DOG?
WHY DOES EACH PRINCE YOU KISS
BECOME A FROG?

DAISY.

I TELL MYSELF, IT'S JUST BAD LUCK
MY FLINGS TURN OUT THIS WAY
BUT WILL THIS PET
EVER GET
THE CHANCE TO SHOUT HOORAY?

PURSE DOGS.

WHY ARE YOU ALWAYS PICKING THE WRONG PUP?
WHY DO YOUR PUGS TURN OUT BE
BIG UGLY MUGS?

DAISY.

BEST IN SHOW, MUTT OR STRAY
I CAN'T GET A ONE OF THOSE DOGS TO STAY
OH, WHY DOES THE WRONG DOG ALWAYS STAY WRONG
AND NEVER GO RIGHT FOR ME?

PURSE DOGS.

COULD IT BE?
A FAULT OF YOUR ANATOMY.
A PROBLEM THAT YOU WON'T ADMIT OR FACE?

COULD IT BE?
THAT YOUR GLUM PERSONALITY
HAS ALL THE TASTE AND GLAMOUR OF TOOTHPASTE?

DAISY.

OH, I STILL DREAM,
AND IN MY DREAMS REALITY
PUTS ON A KINDER FACE,
ONE FULL OF CHARM AND GRACE.

BUT WHEN I WAKE,
I FIND A FLAKE, A LOUSE, A DOLT,
IS SNORING IN MY EAR AND ONCE AGAIN I GET A JOLT.

PURSE DOGS.

> WHY ARE YOU ALWAYS PICKING THE WRONG DOG?
> WHY DOES EACH PRINCE YOU KISS
> BECOME A FROG?

DAISY.

> I TELL MYSELF, IT'S JUST BAD LUCK
> MY FLINGS TURN OUT THIS WAY
> BUT WILL THIS PET
> EVER GET
> THE CHANCE TO SHOUT HOORAY?

PURSE DOGS.

> WHY ARE YOU ALWAYS PICKING THE WRONG PUP?
> WHY DO YOUR PUGS TURN OUT BE
> BIG UGLY MUGS?

DAISY.

> WHERE IS THAT PERFECT PAL, THAT POOCH
> WHO LOVES TO CUDDLE AND PET AND SMOOCH?

ALL.

> OH, WHY DOES THE WRONG DOG ALWAYS STAY WRONG
> AND NEVER GO RIGHT FOR ME?

> (**PURSE DOGS** *exit.*)

DAISY. Get out your crayons and color me gone.

> (**BOGIE** *appears from behind the tree.*)

BOGIE. Daisy, I need to talk to you.

DAISY. Oh, not you, too! Did *everyone* get up on the wrong side of the dog bed?

BOGIE. No, the right side. For the first time in, well…a dog's age.

DAISY. What are you talking about?

BOGIE. You gotta listen to me. I know no one likes a stray.

DAISY. Stray? You?

BOGIE. Boy, you're cute, even when you're playing dumb. But you gotta hear me out.

DAISY. I'm not playing dumb. I had no idea.

BOGIE. I get it. You were mad. Humiliated even. You wanted revenge. And you did the one thing that you knew would hurt me; you turned me in.

DAISY. Wait a minute. I didn't tell anybody a thing about you. In fact, since last week, I haven't thought of you once.

BOGIE. That's a lie.

DAISY. Dog, you're conceited.

BOGIE. I've thought of you a thousand times. Don't tell me you didn't think of me once.

DAISY. Okay. I did think of you. More than once.

BOGIE. That's good news. Just wish you'd paused a little longer, before you ratted me out to your BFF. But I want you to know, I understand.

DAISY. Listen, you. I don't know how or why you got in this mess, but I had nothing to do with it.

BOGIE. I wish I could believe ya.

DAISY. So what's stopping you?

BOGIE. This rope. And…those eyes. A fella could get lost in 'em.

DAISY. *(very close to* **BOGIE***)* Well, take a look at these lips. They're telling the truth.

BOGIE. Nice lips.

DAISY. Thanks.

BOGIE. *(takes* **DAISY** *by the shoulders)* Daisy, listen to me! For the past six months, I've been paralyzed. Waiting for my life to begin again. Then I met you. And everything changed.

DAISY. So, why didn't you say something? I thought you hated me.

BOGIE. Hated you? I –

*(**BOGIE** hesitates, gets an idea, walks to the toy box and pulls out a ukulele)*

SONG #14: I HATE YOU LIKE I HATE ROMANCE

BOGIE.

THESE DAYS WE ALL GET CONFUSED,
NO ONE'S SURE JUST WHAT THE RULES ARE
CONCERNING BOYS AND GIRLS IN LOVE.

BOGIE. *(cont.)*

I'D LIKE TO TELL YOU HOW I FEEL,
BUT THEN I JUST MIGHT REVEAL
EXACTLY WHAT MY HEART IS THINKING OF,
AND SO...

I HATE YOU JUST LIKE I HATE
FRIED POTATOES ON A PLATE,
CHASIN' FIREFLIES TILL IT'S LATE
WITH YOU.

I HATE YOU LIKE I HATE FINE CHEESE,
ROLLING ROUND IN AUTUMN LEAVES,
MOONLIT WALKS ON A SUMMER'S EVE
WITH YOU.

NOW I DON'T KNOW WHY
I CAN'T JUST SAY I LOVE YOU,
BUT 'TIL THAT DAY COMES ALONG,
I'LL STICK
WITH THIS SONG.

I HATE YOU LIKE I HATE ROMANCE,
HEARING MUSIC WHEN WE DANCE,
TAKING A GREAT BIG CHANCE
ON YOU.

(WHISTLE BREAK)

NOW I DON'T KNOW WHY
I CAN'T JUST SAY I LOVE YOU,
BUT 'TIL THAT DAY COMES ALONG,
I'LL STICK
WITH MY SONG.

SOMEDAY I'LL HATE YOU TIL THE SUN COMES UP,
THEN BRING YOU BREAKFAST IN YOUR FAVORITE CUP.
WHO KNOWS? MAYBE I'LL CHANGE MY LUCK
WITH YOU.

(They almost kiss but are interrupted by the sound of an approaching siren.)

(SFX: Distant Siren sound)

*(**CHAMP** and **ITCHY** run on.)*

ITCHY. They're coming!

CHAMP. Animal Control!

DAISY. Animal Control? No!

CHAMP/ITCHY. Bogie! Run for it.

BOGIE. Can't, fellas. I'm a little tied up right now.

DAISY. *(to* **BOGIE***)* How could this happen? Just when we finally… Champ! Do something!

CHAMP. There's nothing we can do. They got wagons on both sides of the park.

ITCHY. *(to himself, wracked with guilt)* Oh, my Dog! What have I done?

DAISY. We need a plan.

BOGIE. A plan is just a list of things that can go wrong. Let's face it. It's curtains for me.

DAISY. Where will they take you? How will we find you?

ITCHY. I know where he's going and it won't be pretty.

SONG #15: THE BIGHOUSE OPERA

CHAMP.

THIS ONE'S GOING TO THE BIGHOUSE!

BOGIE. I know the routine. I been here before. They're wearing uniforms and carrying nets and stun guns.

CHAMP.

THIS ONE'S GOING TO THE BIGHOUSE, SISTER!

BOGIE. They're on walkie-talkies making arrangements. Settin' up guys in trees and on telephone poles.

CHAMP.

THIS ONE'S GOING TO THE BIGHOUSE!

ALL.

SO LONG! FAREWELL! BYE BYE!

(music vamp under lines)

BOGIE. First they hit you with one of those darts, yeah. The kind that leave you slobbering and twitching on the ground. You wanna run but you lie there and take it. Your body's numb but your mind's alive. You hear every word they're sayin'.

ITCHY. I didn't mean it to turn out this way.

ALL.
> THIS ONE'S GOING TO THE BIGHOUSE,
> THIS ONE'S GOING TO THE BIGHOUSE, BROTHER!
> THIS ONE'S GOING TO THE BIGHOUSE,
> SO LONG, FAREWELL, BYE BYE!

BOGIE. They put you in an electric collar, the kind that discourages talking. And with sirens blaring and voices screaming you head for the slammer. As you draw near, you can smell the fear.

ITCHY. I'm a rat, a fink, a stool pigeon!

ALL.
> THIS ONE'S GOING TO THE BIGHOUSE,
> THIS ONE'S GOING TO THE BIGHOUSE, SISTER!
> THIS ONE'S GOING TO THE BIGHOUSE!
> SO LONG, FAREWELL, BYE BYE!

BOGIE. The doors clang open and you're lying on a cold slab of cement. You can barely turn your head, but when you do, you realize you're in a cell, doing time with a mastiff who hasn't been with a dame in 2 years.

ITCHY. This is getting ugly.

ALL.
> THIS ONE'S GOING TO THE BIGHOUSE!
> THIS ONE'S GOING TO THE BIGHOUSE, CHILDREN!
> THIS ONE'S GOING TO THE BIGHOUSE!
> SO LONG, FAREWELL, BYE BYE!

BOGIE. The water bowl is filled with slime and the kibble's covered in mold. No one would eat it.

ITCHY. I would.

CHAMP. Shut up, Itch.

BOGIE. The countdown begins. Two weeks. One. You hope and you pray that someone'll take you outta there, but no one wants a dog with experience. No one wants a life that's been lived. They want pups, with their eyes barely open.

ITCHY. I can't hear any more. *(covers his ears)*

BOGIE. Then you start that long walk down the green mile.

(drum roll)

At the end is a chamber. Yeah, THAT chamber.

(drum roll)

They toss you in. The door clangs shut and you wait –

(drum roll)

counting your heartbeats till the moment when it's over. Lights out.

ALL.

THIS ONE'S GOING TO THE BIGHOUSE!
THIS ONE'S GOING TO THE BIGHOUSE, BROTHER!
THIS ONE'S GOING TO THE BIGHOUSE

CHAMP.

LORDY, LORDY, SAVE HIS SOUL!

DAISY.

TAKE HIM BY THE PAW!

ITCHY.

HI-DEE HI-DEE HO, HI-DEE HI-DEE HAW!

ALL.

SO LONG, FAREWELL, BYE BYE!

(SFX: Loud sirens)

ITCHY. *(hysterical)* Oh my Dog!!

DAISY. We've gotta help Bogie, Champ!

CHAMP. You're right. No dog deserves this.

DAISY. I'll try to undo his leash. You stop the cops.

CHAMP. How?

DAISY. Roll over, play dead. Act, for Dog sakes.

CHAMP. Did you say act???

(SFX: Sirens arrive)

*(**CHAMP** steps into his acting light)*

DAISY. *(to **BOGIE**)* Hold still. I'm trying to set you free.

CHAMP. To be or not to be.

ITCHY. This is agony.

BOGIE. Daisy, hold it. They're expecting to find a dog strung up to this fire hydrant.

CHAMP. Friends, Romans, countrymen.

ITCHY. I can't take it much longer.

DAISY. Oh, Bogie, I'll take your place. I've got a license.

BOGIE. You'd do that for me?

CHAMP. *(Leaps on the toy box and points at* **ITCHY** *in full Shakespearean voice.)* Cry havoc, and let slip the dogs of war!

ITCHY. *(scared out of his mind)* ARRRGH!

CHAMP. *(Grabs* **ITCHY** *and spins him around.)* Turn, hellhound. Turn! I had rather be a dog, and bay the moon, than such a Roman. Cerberus, demon of the pit – CAVE CANEM!

ITCHY. Don't hurt me!

CHAMP. My hounds are bred out of the Spartan kind. Aye, in the catalog ye go for men, as hounds, and greyhounds, mongrels, spaniels, curs, and demi-wolves are clept all by the name of dog!

> *(Pushes* **ITCHY** *down on his knees.)*

Come, kneel upon this molehill here. It is the time when screech owls cry and bane dogs howl. *(howls)*

ITCHY. *(howling)* Okay, I did it! It was me. I ratted Bogie out!

DAISY. Oh, no!

BOGIE. Itch! Why?

ITCHY. I was jealous. I was little. I was a little jealous. You were a sonofabitch. I'm sorry.

CHAMP. Tis Jealousy, the green-eyed monster. Put out the light and then – *(Steps down from toy box.)* Put out the dog.

ITCHY. No! Let me take his place. *(crying)* Please! Let me! Daisy!

DAISY. Itchy, I can't even look at you.

ITCHY. Bogie!

BOGIE. Why should I trust you?

ITCHY. I made a mistake and I'm gonna make it right.

CHAMP. To err is human, to forgive canine.

(SFX: "Spread out men. We're looking for the stray.")

DAISY. *(Gets the knot untied.)* Got it!

BOGIE. All right, Itch. I'm putting my life in your paws.

ITCHY. Thanks, Bogie.

(SFX: "We don't want any trouble.")

ITCHY. (**ITCHY** *puts on* **BOGIE***'s leash.)* You two start running and don't look back.

DAISY. What about you? Your sniffilus?

ITCHY. This is bigger than all of us. Now beat it, you two.

(SFX: Police Whistle)

CHAMP. Itchy! They're here. What do we do now?

ITCHY. Create a distraction.

CHAMP. Ol' Yeller?

ITCHY. *(nods)* The five hanky finish.

(SFX: "That's him! Get the net.")

DAISY. Hide, Bogie! Behind the fence.

BOGIE. *(Catches leg on gate.)* Ow.

(**CHAMP** *goes to the hand sanitizer and puts foam on his mouth. Then he starts growling and snarling, acting the part of Ol' Yeller.)*

CHAMP. ROWL! GRRRWLL!

(SFX: "Oh, my god. We got trouble. Mad Dog! Back up. Back up!" Distorted walkie-talkie "Bring the stun gun" muttering.)

ITCHY. *(Acting the part of Travis.)* Yeller! Here ye are, boy, more grub.

CHAMP. Grrrrr. Stay back!

ITCHY. Yeller! What's the matter, boy?

CHAMP. Don't come near me! *(mad dog growling)* I'm sick.

ITCHY. Yeller, it's me, Travis. You know me.

CHAMP. *(mad dog growling)* I can't control myself. *(growl)* Run! Run away from me. Take little Arliss with you!

ITCHY. Momma! Yeller's sick bad with the rabies. He's sufferin'.

DAISY. *(calls out.)* They've got a gun!

CHAMP. *(mad dog growling.)* Remember our adventures. The good times –

(SFX: Tranquilizer Dart hits **CHAMP** *in the neck.)*

They got me!

BOGIE. Champ's been hit with a tranquilizer dart. We gotta help him.

DAISY. No, Bogie, you can't go out there, they'll recognize you.

CHAMP. *(Speaks in slow motion.)* Re-mem-ber-r-r-r the goo-o-o-d times, Travis. *(Sings the Ole Yeller theme song, fighting to stay conscious. But it finally devolves from a 10 to a 1.)*

OLE YELLER WAS A FIGHTER.
A ROOTIN TOOTIN FIGHTER.
THAT'S HOW A GOOD DOG SHOULD BEEEEE

(Sprawls onto the floor.)

HERE, YELLER. COME BACK, YELLER.
BEST DOGGONE DOG IN THE WEST.

*(***CHAMP*** *passes out.* **ITCHY** *applauds wildly.)*

ITCHY. That was fantastic, Champ. Your best performance ever.

(SFX: Searchlight beam hits **ITCHY** *in the face. He puts up his paws.)*

ITCHY. Not the dart! I'm a bleeder. I'm not a bumblebee. I'm a dog. See? I've got a dog tag. It was all just a joke. I got a million of 'em. What happened when the pitbull went to the flea circus? He stole the show!

(SFX: Dart sound)

Everyone's a critic. Wait! There's more. What do you get when you cross a cocker spaniel, a poodle and a rooster? A cocker-poodle-doo!

(SFX: Dart sound)

ITCHY. *(cont.)* Didn't like that? Okay. How do you catch a runaway dog? Hide behind a tree and make a noise like a bone!

(SFX: 3 dart sounds.)

ITCHY. Missed me. Ha Ha Ha. I'm such a kidder. *(Looks down at* **CHAMP***.)* He's just kidding, too. He's had his shots. Right, Champie? Show 'em you've got a tag and you're okay. *(Wipes hand sanitizer off* **CHAMP***'s face.)* It's just soap. See? Wave good-bye to the nice men, Champster.

CHAMP. *(in a tranquilizer-induced daze)* I'm a princess…

ITCHY. *(Pulls* **CHAMP** *up to sitting position and waves with his paw.)* You missed him. He's totally fine. We're all fine!

CHAMP. *(singing)*

BEST DOGGONE DOG IN THE WEST!

ITCHY. Fine!

(SFX: Grumbling guys. "False alarm. Some kind of prank. Let's get out of here." Shutting of doors. "Loy, you fired 6 shots and missed 6, that's some kind of record. Lay off, Bill." Sound of engines driving off.)

(Dramatic chord, and **ITCHY***, with elaborate vocal gymnastics, pulls off rope and sings.)*

SONG #15G: ITCHY'S REPRISE (THE BIGHOUSE OPERA)

ITCHY.

NO ONE'S GOING TO THE BIG HOUSE!
NO ONE'S GOING TO THE BIGHOUSE. BROTHER!
NO ONE'S GOING TO THE BIG HOUSE!
CHAMP SAVED MY SOUL! BOGIE BEAT THE LAW!
HID-EE HID-EE HEE, HID-EE HID-EE HAW!
I'M HAPPY! SO HAPPY! I COULD CRY.

(During the applause **CHAMP** *wakes up, gets to his feet unsteadily.)*

CHAMP. *(bows)* Thank you. Thank you. I still got it, Itch.

ITCH. Ya sure do, Champ. Best in show!

(**BOGIE** *and* **DAISY** *re-enter.* **BOGIE** *is limping.*)

BOGIE. I caught your act, fellas. Pure gold!

DAISY. You were amazing!

BOGIE. What a team! You saved my gravy.

DAISY. Bogie! Your leg. You're hurt.

(**DAISY** *pulls out a bandana and sits him down to treat his leg.*)

BOGIE. It's nothing. Caught it on the fence –

DAISY. You're bleeding!

BOGIE. *(notices the bandana)* Say, where'd you get that bandana?

DAISY. It belonged to my best friend's fiancé. Never met him. It was before my time. Let me help you –

BOGIE. *(catches her hand.)* What happened to him?

DAISY. It's a sad story. She must have told it to me a thousand times. Hold still. You see, he'd been gone for nearly a year, on tour with –

BOGIE. *(Taking bandana and looks at it closely.)* – his band?

DAISY. *(surprised)* Yeah, that's right. He returned to town the end of October –

BOGIE. October twenty second.

DAISY. *(Looks at him for a moment, then continues.)* Yes. And they had a date at the top of the Space Needle, where they'd met nearly 2 years before.

BOGIE. It was cold that day and –

(Underscoring [Replay Bogie's Somewhere])

DAISY & BOGIE. – snowy.

(They look at each other.)

BOGIE. Which was rare.

DAISY. He said –

BOGIE. "Bogie, stay here, will ya, pal? I'm gonna see my girl."

DAISY. He'd meet her at five.

BOGIE. "And I'll be back in two hours."

DAISY. She was at the top of the Space Needle at 4:30.

BOGIE. *(looks out)* So I waited.

DAISY. At five PM she heard sirens. She looked down at the street, ambulances were everywhere. She saw a body. It was him.

BOGIE. My friend.

DAISY. She was frantic to get to him. She waited for the elevator but it was too slow.

BOGIE. My best friend.

DAISY. She took the stairs three at time, kicking off her heels and running in her bare feet. She reached him as they were loading him into the ambulance.

(**ITCHY** *and* **CHAMP** *listen intently.*)

BOGIE. I kept waiting.

DAISY. All he was able to say was –

BOGIE. "Stay. I'll be back for you."

DAISY. He didn't see the car. He was looking up. He pressed that bandana into her hand.

BOGIE. Then he was gone.

DAISY. Oh, Bogie. I'm so sorry.

BOGIE. The not knowing was the hard part.

ITCHY. That's the saddest story I ever heard.

BOGIE. So long, pal.

(*silence*)

Well… I guess I don't have to hang around here anymore.

DAISY. Now wait a minute. You can't just go off and lick your wounds by yourself.

CHAMP. Daisy's right. This is no time to be alone.

ITCHY. Your pack needs you.

DAISY. And I think you need us.

BOGIE. Spare me the cheap sentiment.

DAISY. Come on, Bogie, you have to see this was fate. *Your* best friend and *my* best friend…?

CHAMP. It's in the stars.

ITCHY. Personally, I've never had my day, but this could be yours, Boge.

BOGIE. Baloney.

SONG #16: STAY WITH ME

(INTRO begins.)

DAISY. Aw, Bogie, you don't have to keep up the tough guy act with me.

(sings)

I KNOW HOW YOU HATE THINGS SENTIMENTAL,
SO I'LL TAKE THIS SLOW AND INCREMENTAL,
SEE HOW "ME"
AND "YOU" MAKES "WE"
AND –

DAISY/ITCHY/CHAMP.

STAY WITH ME.

DAISY.

WHY DONCHA, HUH?

*(**BOGIE** crosses to tree to get his stuff. **DAISY** follows.)*

DAISY.

FUNNY HOW THIS FEELS SO ACCIDENTAL,
YET HERE WE ARE IN SOMETHING TRANSCENDENTAL.
CAN'T YOU SEE
WE'RE MEANT TO BE
SO –

DAISY/ITCHY/CHAMP.

STAY WITH ME

DAISY.

AND WE CAN

DAISY/ITCHY/CHAMP.

SLIDE

DAISY.

SLIDE RIGHT OVER THE MOON
TO SPOON.

DAISY/ITCHY/CHAMP.

GLIDE

DAISY.

    LIKE FRED AND GINGER –

ITCHY & CHAMP.

    OR TRAMP AND LADY –

DAISY.

    IT'S YOU AND ME, BABY!

DAISY/ITCHY/ CHAMP.

    JUST BEFORE YOU THINK THAT WE'VE GONE MENTAL,

    DON'T YOU GO AND BE SO DARN JUDGEMENTAL.

CHAMP.

    LISTEN TO ME,

ITCHY.

    AND YOU'LL AGREE TO

DAISY/ITCHY/CHAMP.

    STAY WITH ME.

    *(**DAISY** and **BOGIE** dance. **ITCHY** and **CHAMP** exit.)*

BOGIE. When did you know?

DAISY. I know what?

BOGIE. How you felt about me.

DAISY. That's easy. You had me at woof.

    *(**BOGIE** smiles and spins her.)*

DAISY.

    I'VE BEEN FOOLED BEFORE BY HANDSOME FACES.

BOGIE.

    THEN I WAS BEGUILED BY YOUR SWEET GRACES.

DAISY & BOGIE.

    SEE HOW "YOU"

    AND "ME" MAKE "TWO,"

    AND STAY WITH ME.

DAISY.

    WHY CAN'T YA, HUH?

BOGIE.

    MAYBE I'VE BEEN SEARCHING IN WRONG PLACES,

    THEN YOU SHOWED YOUR HAND WITH ALL THE ACES.

DAISY.

    CAN'T YOU SEE ?

BOGIE.

WE'RE MEANT TO BE.

DAISY & BOGIE.

SO STAY WITH ME.

*(***PURSE DOGS*** appear, operated by* **CHAMP** *and* **ITCHY**.*)*

PURSE DOGS.

AND WE CAN DREAM

DAISY.

DREAM OF PUPS OF OUR OWN
AT HOME.

PURSE DOGS.

IT SEEMS

BOGIE.

WE'RE PERFECT TOGETHER

DAISY.

LIKE PEACHES AND FUZZ,

PURSE DOGS.

LIKE WOODY AND BUZZ.

BOGIE & DAISY.

THINK HOW WE'D BEHAVE IN OPEN SPACES,
NO ONE NEAR TO SEE OUR FOND EMBRACES.

DAISY.

LISTEN TO ME,

BOGIE.

AND YOU'LL AGREE,

ALL.

PLEASE,
STAY WITH ME.

*(***PURSE DOGS*** exit.*)*

DAISY. Say, Bogie, do you like gardens?

BOGIE. Who doesn't.

DAISY. Ours blooms year round.

BOGIE. Nice.

(They kiss.)

(SFX: PA VOICE: "It's Yappy Hour. Keep it clean.")

BOGIE. Yappy Hour! I can already hear the tails waggin'.

(SFX: PA VOICE: "So fetch a friend and join us on the green.")

(ITCHY and CHAMP enter.)

ITCHY. Yappy Hour. The best time of day.

(Music starts as ITCHY returns with fire hydrant cocktail shaker and little dog bowls.)

BOGIE. *(Raises a bowl in toast to DAISY.)* Here's looking at you, kid!

DAISY. *(to audience)* I love yappy endings.

ITCHY. *(raising his bowl to CHAMP)* Remember, when you lie down with dogs, you wake up with dogs.

CHAMP. That's deep, Itch.

ITCHY. I know.

(ANNOUNCER: "It's time to gather round for the hottest dance in all downtown – the Two Dog Trot!")

(The group sets down their bowls, and sings and swing dances.)

SONG #17: TWO DOG TROT

BOGIE.
THERE'S A LITTLE DANCE THAT WE ALL KNOW,
WE DO IT IN THE PLACE WHERE WE ALL GO.
EARLY IN THE EVENING WHEN THE SUN GOES DOWN
EVERY STRAY COMES FROM MILES AROUND
IT'S NEVER TOO HOT – TO DO THE TWO DOG TROT.

ITCHY.
WELL, YOU CAN ALLEMAND LEFT,

CHAMP.
YOU CAN SASHAY RIGHT,

ITCHY.
ONE THING FOR SURE, YOU'RE GONNA DANCE ALL NIGHT.

CHAMP.
NO NEED TO LOOK FOR A RHYME OR REASON,

ITCHY.
ONE THING FOR SURE, IT'S ALWAYS THE SEASON,

ITCHY/CHAMP.

AND NEVER TOO HOT – TO DO THE TWO DOG TROT.

ALL.

TWO DOG TROT!

DAISY.

YOU'RE SEEIN' DOUBLE.

ALL.

TWO DOG TROT!

BOGIE.

LOOKIN' FOR TROUBLE.

ALL.

TWO DOG TROT!

ITCHY.

NO RHYME, NOR REASON.

ALL.

TWO DOG TROT!

CHAMP.

ALWAYS IN SEASON

ALL.

AND NEVER TOO HOT – TO DO THE TWO DOG TROT!

ITCHY/CHAMP.

DOO DOO DOO-DO-DOO

DOO DOO DOO-DOO-DOO!

DOO DOO DOO-DOO DOO

DOO DOO DOO-DOO-DOO

DE-DOO DOO DOO DOO DOO DOO DOODLE DOO DEE DAH DAH

CHAMP. Looks like it's you and me, Itch.

ITCHY. But I'm a boy. In a bee suit.

CHAMP. *(shrugs)* Nobody's perfect.

ALL.

TWO DOG TROT!

DAISY.

YOU'RE SEEIN' DOUBLE.

ALL.

TWO DOG TROT!

BOGIE.

LOOKIN' FOR TROUBLE.

ALL.

TWO DOG TROT!

ITCHY.

NO RHYME, NOR REASON.

ALL.

TWO DOG TROT!

CHAMP.

ALWAYS IN SEASON

ALL.

AND NEVER TOO HOT – TO DO THE TWO DOG TROT!

BOGIE. One more time!

ALL.

TWO DOG TROT!

DAISY.

YOU'RE SEEIN' DOUBLE.

ALL.

TWO DOG TROT!

BOGIE.

LOOKIN' FOR TROUBLE.

ALL.

TWO DOG TROT!

ITCHY.

NO RHYME, NOR REASON.

ALL.

TWO DOG TROT!

CHAMP.

ALWAYS IN SEASON

ALL.

AND NEVER TO HOT – TO DO THE TWO DOG TROT!

End of Play

DOGPARK SET and PROP LIST

Dogpark takes place in an urban setting. The script specifies Seattle but it could be changed to any other city. The park has a chain link fence that defines its area. Behind it and all around it we see the City. The park needs to have at least one tree – Bogie's Tree, a bench under that tree, a gate that swings or slides open to allow the dogs to enter and exit, a bulletin board with events and times posted for the day's events, a toy box, a trash can, and, of course, a fire hydrant. There should be a place for the purse dog puppets (or people) to appear – behind the bulletin board, over a fence or out from behind the tree. The song "Today is the Day" is performed as if the dogs are in cars. Car windows or steering wheels have been used in past productions.

ACT I
Prop Pre-set:
Rubber chicken without squeaker
Stick
Fire hydrant
Big rawhide bone
Dog biscuit
Ball
Cat toy (in Bogie's pocket)
Bandana that belonged to Bogie's owner, tied around Daisy's wrist (costume)
Oversized man's jacket (that belonged to Bogie's owner, the rock musician)
Hand sanitizer, attached to bulletin board or trashcan
Poop scoop bags attached to trashcan or bulletin board
Grass clippings that Itchy pretends to eat

Inside Toy Box:
Shoe that's been chewed
Ball on rope

Offstage:
Frisbee
Note with 3 paw prints (big enough to be seen by audience)
Actor side (5x7 page that Champ pulls out of his pocket)
4 workout poles with red and white stripes
3 Purse Dog puppets – a Chihuahua, a Yorkie and a Pug (alternatively, could also be played by actors in some kind of head gear)

ACT II
Trashcan with red light (to signify a fire) and a little trash
10-12 ft. rope, one end loosely noosed to go around Bogie's neck, the other to attach to fence or fire hydrant
A working ukelele (preset in toybox during intermission)
Tray with fire hydrant cocktail shaker and 4 small dog bowls

COSTUMES

The costumes should represent what dogs would wear if they were people at a singles bar. Dog ears are a nice touch with fur elements included at collars and cuffs. Their outfit is them, so a dog wouldn't take off his jacket. Itchy's Best Friend dresses him in sweaters, workout gear and a bumble bee costume over his clothes. In the "Gotta Pick Me" speed mating scene, each actor plays another dog besides his/her character. This can be represented by headbands with hair and ears, or face-sized hand mirror frames with hair and ears attached to the circular rim. The actors hold the mask up to their faces to create the new character.

DAISY
White Westie – sexy
Collar with tag
Bandanna that matches Bogie's (House of Blues)
    Debbie Downer Basset – long bassett ears and a bow

BOGIE
Lab/mutt – dark and mysterious: Beat-up leather jacket, dark tee, dark jeans with tears and patches, biker boots, fingerless gloves
No collar or tag
Bandanna that matches Daisy's.
    Ginger: Afghan Hound
        Long haired wig
        Furry boots
        Short skirt
        Heels or tennis shoes (it is agility class!)
    Sheepdog: Shaggy ears and bangs on headband or mask

CHAMP
Collie show dog – vain and glorious. Tight pants, jacket with fur ruff
Collar and tag
    Trix: Poodle
        Pom pom poodle wig
        Spandex tights,
        Short skirt
        Heels or tennis shoes
    Brutus: Pit bull junk yard dog, missing an eye and an ear
        Eye patch

ITCHY
Jack Russell – neurotic spotted dog. Turtleneck with spots, corduroy pants, saddle shoes
Collar and tag
Sweater vest with lettered "Hot Dog" on chest in first act
Nylon basketball shorts and tank top jersey and headband for Agility Class
Bumble Bee costume with antenna and wings in Act II
    Skank: Chinese crested Chihuahua
        Spotted with hair tied up in a messy top pony tail

Also by

Jahnna Beecham &
Malcolm Hilgartner

Chaps!

Chaps!
A Jingle Jangle Christmas!

OTHER TITLES AVAILABLE FROM SAMUEL FRENCH

CHAPS!
Jahnna Beecham and Malcolm Hilgartner

Musical Comedy / 5m, 1f / Unit Set

Whoa, Brittania! Panic at the BBC! The year is 1944, America's favorite singing cowboy Tex Riley and his troupe are late for a special broadcast at the BBC in London. Out of desperation, Mabel, their tour manager, and Miles, the frantic young producer, grab whomever they can — a snobby announcer, an amiable sound man, a passing soap opera actor — slap them into costume, hand them scripts (after all, it's radio!) and shove them in front of the studio audience. The resulting performance is one England will never forget. Also available in a special holiday version, *Chaps! A Jingle Jangle Christmas.*

"...A rootin' tootin' good time... as wholesomely western as a festival of Gene Autry movies."
— *North County Times*

"Just the ticket to take away the blues."
— KPBS, San Diego

"Opening night standing ovation!"
— *The Reader*

"...A hoot...entertaining hoedown."
— *Seattle Times*

"...Rustles up a stampede of old-time radio nostalgia and campy humor."
— *Seattle Post-Intelligencer*

\\

OTHER TITLES AVAILABLE FROM SAMUEL FRENCH

CHAPS! A JINGLE JANGLE CHRISTMAS
Jahnna Beecham and Malcolm Hilgartner

Holiday Musical Comedy / 5m, 2f / Unit Set

In this follow up to the wildly7 sucessful CHAPS! The musical, the chap's gang is reunited for on Christmas Eve, 1944. Watch as cowboy Tex Riley and his troupe stumble and tumble there way through their Christmas broadcast. A perfect show for any and all theatres looking to spread Holiday Cheer–BBC style!

"…Combine Monty Python and Tex Ritter, and you get a bloody funny singing buckaroo!"
— *Herald News*

"Beautiful harmony…sparkling energy…exquisitely timed…an endearing production."
— *Milwaukee Journal Sentinel*

"...Ropes in the audience with plenty of laughs."
— *The San Diego Union-Tribune*

"Winning performances!"
— *Los Angeles Times*

OTHER TITLES AVAILABLE FROM SAMUEL FRENCH

DON'T HUG ME
Book and Lyrics by Phil Olson. Music by Paul Olson.

Musical Comedy / 3m, 2f / Int.

It's *Fargo* meets *The Music Man*
(without the blood or the trombones).

Oh, for cryin' in yer snow shoes! It's the coldest day of the year in Bunyan Bay when a slick karaoke salesman arrives at the bar and turns the locals' lives upside down. With its over the top songs and crazy characters, this "Minnesota love story with singin' and stuff" will have you laughing until the spring thaw!

Don't Hug Me takes place in Bunyan Bay, Minnesota. Cantankerous bar owner, Gunner Johnson, wants to sell the business and move to Florida. Clara, his wife and former Winter Carnival Bunyan Queen, wants to stay. Bernice Lundstrom, the pretty waitress, wants to pursue a singing career. Her fiance, Kanute Gunderson, wants her to stay home. It's a battle of wills, and when a fast-talking salesman, Aarvid Gisselsen, promises to bring romance into their lives through the 'magic' of karaoke, all heck breaks loose!

Featuring the songs, *"I'm a Walleye Woman in a Crappie Town,"*
"My Smorgasbord of Love," and *"I Wanna Go to the Mall of America."*

"A hokey jokey karaoke crowd pleaser!"
- Los Angeles Times

"A lot of laughs!...A great time! Go see it!"
- Tom Barnard, KQRS